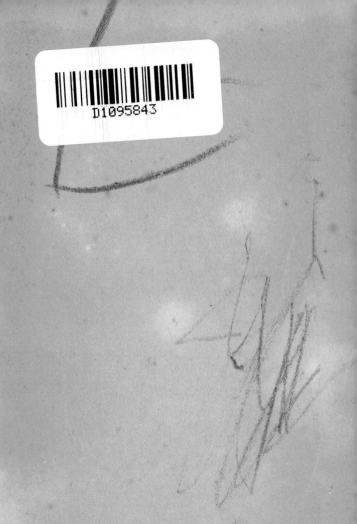

The Uncrowned King

By

HAROLD BELL WRIGHT

Author of
"The Shepherd of the Hills"
etc., etc.

**Illustrations
By John Rea Neill**

The Book Supply Company
Publishers, Chicago

To

MR. ELSBERY W. REYNOLDS

My

Publisher and Friend,

Whose belief in my work has made my

work possible, I gratefully

dedicate this tale

of

The Uncrowned King

Redlands, California,
       May fourth, 1910

"Eyes blinded by the fog of Things cannot see Truth. Ears deafened by the din of Things cannot hear Truth. Brains bewildered by the whirl of Things cannot think Truth. Hearts deadened by the weight of Things cannot feel Truth. Throats choked by the dust of Things cannot speak Truth."

CONTENTS

ILLUSTRATIONS
Drawn by
John Rea Neill

The Pilgrim and His Pilgrimage

The Pilgrim and His Pilgrimage

FOR many, many, weary
months the Pilgrim jour-
neyed in the wide and

pathless Desert of Facts. So many
indeed were the months that the
wayworn Pilgrim, himself, came at
last to forget their number.

And always, for the Pilgrim, the
sky by day was a sky of brass,
softened not by so much as a
wreath of cloud mist. Always, for
him, the hot air was stirred not by
so much as the lift of a wild bird's
wing. Never, for him, was the
awful stillness of the night broken
by voice of his kind, by foot-fall
of beast, or by rustle of creeping
thing. For the toiling Pilgrim in
the vast and pathless Desert of
Facts there was no kindly face,
no friendly fire. Only the stars

were many—many and very near.

Day after day, as the Pilgrim labored onward, through the torturing heat, under the sky of brass, he saw on either hand lakes of living waters and groves of many palms. And the waters called him to their healing coolness: the palms beckoned him to their restful shade and shelter. Night after night, in the dreadful solitude, frightful Shapes came on silent feet out of the silent darkness to stare at him with doubtful, questioning, threatening eyes; drawing back at last, if he stood still, as silently as they had come, or, if he advanced, vanishing quickly, only to reappear as silently in another place.

But the Pilgrim knew that the enchanting scenes that lured him by day were but pictures in the heated air. He knew that the fearful Shapes that haunted him by night were but creatures of his own overwrought fancy. And so he journeyed on and ever on, in the staggering heat, under the sky of brass, in the awful stillness of the night: on and ever on, through the wide and pathless waste, until he came at last to the Outer-Edge-Of-Things—came to the place that is between the Desert of Facts and the Beautiful Sea, even as it is written in the Law of the Pilgrimage.

The tired feet of the Traveler left now the rough, hot floor of the desert for a soft, cool carpet of velvet grass all inwrought with blossoms that filled the air with fragrance. Over his head, tall trees gently shook their glistening, shadowy leaves, while sweet voiced birds of rare and wondrous plumage flitted from bough to bough. Across a sky of deepest blue, fleets of fairy cloud ships, light as feathery down, floated—floated—drifting lazily, as though, piloted only by the wind, their pilot slept. All about him, as he walked, multitudes of sunlight and shadow fairies danced gaily hand in hand. And over the shimmering surface of the Sea a thousand thousand fairy waves ran joyously, one after the other, from the sky line to the pebbly beach, making liquid music clearer and softer than the softest of clear toned bells.

And there it was, in that wondrously beautiful place, the Outer-Edge-Of-Things, that the Pilgrim found, fashioned of sheerest white, with lofty dome, towering spires, and piercing minarets lifting out of the living green, the Temple of Truth.

In reverent awe the Pilgrim

stood before the sacred object of his Pilgrimage.

At last, with earnest step, the worshiper approached the holy edifice. But when he would have passed through the high arched door, his way was barred by one whose garments were white even as the whiteness of the Temple, whose eyes were clear even as the skies, and whose face shone even as the shining Beautiful Sea.

The Pilgrim, hesitating, spoke: "You are?"

The other answered in a voice that was even as the soft wind that stirred the leaves of the forest: "I am Thyself."

Then the Pilgrim—"And your office?"

"I am the appointed Keeper of the Temple of Truth; save by my permission none may enter here."

Cried the Pilgrim eagerly: "But I? I may enter? Surely I have fulfilled The Law! Surely I have paid The Price!"

"What law have you fulfilled? What price have you paid?" gently asked he in the garments of white.

Proudly now the other answered: "I have accomplished alone the long journey through the Desert of Facts. Alone I have endured the days under the sky of brass; alone I have borne the awful solitude of the nights. I was not drawn aside by the lovely scenes that tempted me. I was not turned back by the dreadful Shapes that threatened me. And so I have attained the Outer-Edge-Of-Things."

"You have indeed fulfilled The Law," said he of the shining face. "And The Price?"

The Pilgrim answered sadly: "I left behind all things dearest to the heart of man—Wealth of Traditions inherited from the Long Ago, Holy Prejudices painfully gathered through the ages of the past, Sacred Opinions, Customs,

Favors and Honors of the World
that is, in the times that are."

"You have indeed paid The
Price," said the soft voice of the
other, "but still, still there is one
thing more."

"And the one thing more?"
asked the Pilgrim, "I knew not
that there could be one thing
more."

The Keeper of the Temple was
silent for a little, then said very
gently: "Is there nothing, O Hadji,
that you would ask Thyself?"

Then all at once the Pilgrim
understood. Said he slowly:
"There is still one thing more.
Tell me, tell me—Why? Why

The Law of the Pilgrimage? Why the journey so long? Why the way so hard? Why is the Temple of Truth here on the Outer-Edge-Of-Things?"

And Thyself answered clearly: "He who lives always within Things can never worship in Truth. Eyes blinded by the fog of Things cannot see Truth. Ears deafened by the din of Things cannot hear Truth. Brains bewildered by the whirl of Things cannot think Truth. Hearts deadened by the weight of Things cannot feel Truth. Throats choked by the dust of Things cannot speak Truth. Therefore, O Hadji, is the Temple of Truth here on the Outer-Edge-Of-Things; therefore is The Law of the Pilgrimage."

"And The Price?" asked the Pilgrim; "It was so great a price. Why?"

Thyself answered: "Found you no bones in the Desert? Found you no graves by the way?"

The other replied: "I saw the Desert white with bones—I found the way set among many graves."

"And the hands of the dead?"—asked Thyself, in that voice so like the wind that stirred the leaves of the forest—"And the hands of the dead?"

And the Pilgrim answered now

with understanding: "The hands of the dead held fast to their treasures—held fast to their Wealth of Traditions, to their Holy Prejudices, to the Sacred Opinions, Customs, Favors and Honors of Men."

Then Thyself, the appointed Keeper of the Temple of Truth, went quietly aside from the path. With slow and reverent step, with bowed uncovered head, the Pilgrim crossed the threshold and through the high arched doorway entered the sacred corridors.

But within the Temple, before approaching the altar with his offering, the Pilgrim was constrained to retire to The Quiet Room, there to spend the hours until a new day in prayerful meditation. It was there that this Tale of The Uncrowned King came to him—came to him at the end of his long pilgrimage across the Desert of Facts—came to him after he had paid The Price, after he had fulfilled The Law, after he had asked of Thyself, the Keeper of the Temple, "Why?"

There, in The Quiet Room in the Temple of Truth on the Outer-Edge-Of-Things, the Voices to the Pilgrim told this Tale of The Uncrowned King.

And the First Voice was the
Voice of the Waves

And the First Voice was the Voice of the Waves

IT was nearing the fall of day
when first the Pilgrim laid
himself to meditate upon his
couch in The Quiet Room.

Without the Temple, **the tall**

trees rustled softly their glossy leaves and over the flower-figured carpet of green the sunlight and shadow fairies danced along the lanes of gold. High in the blue above, the fairy cloud-fleets were drifting—drifting—idly floating. Over the Beautiful Sea, the glad wave fairies ran one after the other from beyond the far horizon to the sandy shore.

In The Quiet Room where the Pilgrim lay, it was very, very, still. Only the liquid music of the waves came through the open window — came to the Pilgrim clearer and sweeter than the sweetest notes from clear toned bells.

And after a little there was in the music of the waves a Voice.

Said the Voice: "To thee, O Hadji, I come from the Beautiful Sea; the interminable, unfathomable sea, that begins at the Outer-Edge-Of-Things and stretches away into Neverness. I speak from out the Deeps Beneath. I tell of the Great That Is. I am a Voice of Life, O Hadji, and mine it is to begin for you The Tale of The Uncrowned King."

And this is the beginning of the Tale that the Voice of the Waves began.

Very great and very wonderful, O Hadji, is the Land of Allthetime.

Very great and very wonderful is the Royal City Daybyday. Beautiful in Allthetime are the lakes and rivers, the mountains, plains and streams. Beautiful in Daybyday are the groves and gardens, the drives and parks, the harbors and canals. Countless, in this Royal City, are the palaces. Without number are the people—without number and of many races, languages, and names.

But amid the countless palaces in this marvelous city Daybyday, there is one Temple only—only one. For the numberless people of the many races, languages, and names, there is but one God—only one. About this Royal City there is no Wall. For the King of Allthetime, who dwells in Daybyday, there is no Crown.

But the days that were were not as the days that are, O Hadji, and therefore is this Tale.

In the long ago olden days, when King What-Soever-Youthink ruled over the Land of Allthetime, there were, in this Royal City Daybyday, religions many — as many quite as the races, languages and names of the people. Many then were the temples built by the many followers of the many religions to their many gods. For you must know that King What-Soever-Youthink was, of all wise kings that ever were or will be, the very wisest and, therefore, permitted his subjects to worship whom they would.

Always in the city streets there were vast throngs of people passing to and fro among the temples, bearing offerings and singing praises to the gods of their choice; for the chiefest occupation of the dwellers in Daybyday was then, as it is now, the old, old, occupation of worship. Some of the temples, it is true, were at times quite deserted, while in others there was not room for the multitudes; but even in the nearly empty temples the priests and beggars always remained, for, in that age, the people of Daybyday changed often their gods nor followed any very far.

And you must know, too, O Hadji, that in those long ago olden days — the days of the reign of What-Soever-Youthink there was for the Ruler of Allthetime a Crown; and that of all the wonders in that wonderful land this Crown was the most wonderful. More dear to the people of Daybyday than their city itself, more precious than their splendid temples, more sacred even than their many gods, was this—the Crown of their King.

It was so, first, because the Crown was extremely old. From the beginning of the reign of the the Royal Family Everyone, no one knows how many thousands of ages ago, it had passed from king to king, even until that day.

It was so, second, because the Crown was exceedingly valuable. From the very beginning of the beginning each ruler had in turn added a jewel to the golden, gem encrusted emblem of his rank.

It was so, third, because the Crown was a Magic Crown, though no one then knew its magic—they knew only that its magic was.

Therefore, again, O Hadji, is this Tale.

[42]

Also, in those days, there was about this Royal City a Wall—a wall built, so they said, on the very foundations of the world; so strong that no force could breach it, and so high that the clouds often hid its towers and battlements. Only from the topmost cupola of the Royal Palace could one see over this mighty barrier. Only by the Two Great Gates could one pass through.

And so the good people of Allthetime could all quite clearly see that in the Royal City Daybyday the precious Magic Crown was as safe as ever crown could be. And it was so, O Hadji—it was so. The Crown was as safe as ever crown could be—as safe indeed as ever a crown can be.

And this too is truth, O Hadji; that in Daybyday, even now, you may find ruins of the many temples, and here and there a little of the many gods. Even now you may see where the Great Wall was. But of the Crown, in these days, there is nothing— nothing.

And this is how it happened— this is the way it came to be.

King What-Soever-Youthink was the father of two sons; twins they were, and their names—Really-Is and Seemsto-Be. No one in all the kingdom could tell them one from the other, though the princes themselves knew that Really-Is was first born, and that when the wise king, their father, died, it would be for him to occupy the throne, to wear the Crown, and rule the Land of Allthetime.

One day when the young princes were playing in the palace yard they discovered, by chance, an old door that led to the stairway in a tower. Of course they climbed up, up, up, until they stood at last in the cupola at the very top. Far beneath their feet they saw the roofs of the Royal Palace, and the gardens, fields, and orchards, like spots and splashes of color. The walks and courts appeared as lines and squares of white, while the soldiers and servants moved about like tiny animated dots. Reaching away from the palace grounds on every side was the wonderful city Daybyday, so far below that no sound could reach their ears. To their delight, the princes found that they could even look down upon the Great Wall; and, because there were that day no clouds to shut out the view, they could see far, far away over the Land of Allthetime.

"Look, brother," cried Seemsto-Be, catching Really-Is by the arm

in quick excitement, "Look! what is that flashing and gleaming in the sun?"

As he spoke, he pointed afar off to the land beyond the river that marks the end of Allthetime.

"I'm sure I cannot tell;" answered Really-Is, shading his eyes with his open hand and gazing long and earnestly in the direction his brother indicated; "It looks—it looks like a city."

"It is, it is," cried Seemsto-Be. "It is the City Sometime in the Land of Yettocome. I remember hearing once the Chief Gardener telling the Chief Coachman about

it, and he said that the Chief Cook
said that he heard the Captain of
the Guard say that it is far more
wonderful than our own city Daybyday; and it must be so, Really-
Is, for see, brother, how the walls
shine like polished silver, and look!
Is not that a palace or a temple
blazing so like a ruby flame?"

Often after that did the twin
princes, Really-Is and Seemsto-Be,
climb the winding stairs in the
palace tower and look away over
the Great Wall of Daybyday to the
City Sometime in the Land of Yettocome. Many were the hours
they spent talking of the marvelous place that so filled the distance

with dazzling splendor. And at last, when the princes were quite grown, they went before their royal father and asked permission to visit the city they had seen.

Now King What-Soever-You-think was very sad when his sons made their request, but nevertheless, because he was a wise king, he gave his royal consent, and, that the brothers might make their journey in comfort, presented to each a priceless horse from the palace stables. To Really-Is he gave Reality; to Seemsto-Be he gave Appearance; and both were steeds of noble breeding, swift and strong, beautiful and proud—as like even as the royal twins, their masters.

So it came that the two princes bade farewell to their father, the King, and rode bravely out of the city Daybyday, through the Land of Allthetime, and along the way that leads to the City Sometime in the Land of Yettocome.

"And this, O Hadji," said the Voice of the Waves, "is all of The Tale of The Uncrowned King that is given me to tell."

The liquid music of the waves came no longer through the open window—the voice that was in the music came no more to the Pilgrim in The Quiet Room. Without the

Temple the tall trees were still—still and silent were the sweet-voiced birds. The sunlight and shadow fairies had danced to the ends of the lanes of gold—danced to the very ends and were gone. The feathery cloud ships in the blue above seemed to lie at anchor, and over the surface of the Beautiful Sea no laughing ripples ran to play on the pebbly beach.

The Pilgrim arose from his couch, and, going to the open window, looked, and there, in the still, fathomless, depth of the clear water, he saw as in a crystal glass the wonderful city Daybyday with its canals and harbors, its parks and

And the Second Voice was the
Voice of the Evening Wind

*And the Second Voice was
the Voice of the Evening Wind*

IT was early twilight when the
Pilgrim in The Quiet Room
returned to his couch and to
his meditations.

Without the Temple, the last of the day was stealing over the rim of the world into the mysterious realm of the yesterdays. The feathery cloud ships no longer floated white in the depth of blue, but with wide flung sails of rose and crimson swept over an ocean of amethyst and gold. The ripples that ran on the Beautiful Sea were edged with yellow and scarlet flame, while leaf, and blade, and flower, and bird, and all of their kind and kin, were singing their evensong. Sweetly, softly, the choral anthem stole through the open window into The Quiet Room.

And after a little the Pilgrim heard, whispering low, in the twilight hymn, the Voice of the Evening Wind.

Said the Voice: "To thee, O Hadji, I come from the Boundless Ocean Above that begins wherever you are and extends farther away than the farthest point your thought can reach. I speak from out the Deeps Beyond. I tell of the Great That May Be. I too am a Voice of Life and mine it is to continue for you The Tale of The Uncrowned King."

And this is the part of the Tale that was told by the Voice of the Evening Wind.

The twin princes Really-Is and
Seemsto-Be, on their good horses
Reality and Appearance, journeyed
very pleasantly through the Land
of Allthetime toward the City
Sometime in the Land of Yettocome. Ever as they went the
Royal travelers saw before them
the walls of the city gleaming like
polished silver in the sun, and high
above the shining walls the great
palace or temple that flamed like
a ruby flame. Always as they
rode the two talked gaily, in glad
anticipation of the marvels they
would certainly see, of the pleasures they would surely find, and
of the delightful adventures that

without doubt awaited them. So at last they arrived at the city gate, which was a gate all scrolled and patterned with precious gems.

Fairer than the dreams of angels, O Hadji, is the City Sometime in the Land of Yettocome. Of such radiant splendors, such dazzling brilliancy, such transcending glory there are yet no words fashioned to tell. It is a city, in the form and manner of its building, of exquisite loveliness, of fairy grace, of towering grandeur. It is a city in the beauty and richness of its color, all emerald, rose, and purple, all ruby, crimson and gold.

As the twin princes of Allthe-

time rode slowly through the wide
jeweled gate and along the noble
streets and stately avenues, they
exclaimed aloud with delight and
wonder at the enchanting beauty
of the scene. More than they had
heard at home was true. The
poorest of the buildings in Sometime far exceeded in splendor the
richest of the palaces in Daybyday;
while before the palaces of Sometime, Really-Is and Seemsto-Be
stood speechless and amazed. They
were fairly drunken with the flashing, flaming, blazing, blinding glory
of the sight.

The people of Sometime, too,
were exceeding fair and very charm-

ing in their manner, and they wel-
comed the princes from Daybyday
with a joyous welcome, answering
their questions gladly and es-
corting them to the palace of their
king. For you must know, O
Hadji, that the City Sometime,
too, is a Royal City, the home of
Lookingahead, who rules over the
Land of Yettocome. And King
Lookingahead received his noble
visitors with gladness and had
great pleasure, he said, in present-
ing them to his two daughters, the
princesses of Yettocome, Fancy
and Imagination, who were fairer
than any women the princes of
Daybyday had ever seen, even

in the loveliest of their dreams.

For a long happy, happy time Really-Is and Seemsto-Be remained in the City Sometime. Every day, and every day, with the royal princesses Fancy and Imagination for their guides, they rode or drove through the wide streets and broad avenues, walked in the beautiful gardens, explored the shadowy groves or visited the many palaces. And in this way it was that the charming princesses showed to their noble guests all the wonders of the Royal City of the Realm of Yettocome, pointing out for them every day new beauties, finding for them always new pleasures, leading them ever to fresh scenes of enchanting loveliness. And in turn the princes told their fair guides many things of their own city, Daybyday, in the Land of Allthetime; of the people with their many temples and their many gods; of their father What-Soever-Youthink and his wise reign. But most of all did they tell of the wonderful Crown, so very old, so very valuable, and how it was a Magic Crown, though no one then knew its magic, but knew only that its magic was.

Thus Really-Is and Seemsto-Be learned that the dwellers in Sometime were unlike the people of

Daybyday in many ways, but in no way more than this, that they worshiped one god only, only one. The temple sacred to this god stood in the very heart of the city, which is the very heart of the land, and it was this temple, blazing like a ruby flame high above the shining city walls, the princes had seen from the tower of their palace home.

Often, very often did the four young people visit this shrine in Sometime with rich offerings to the god, Itmightbe.

But there came a time at last when, returning from a long ramble through the city, Really-Is and Seemsto-Be were met at the palace door by a royal messenger from home with the word that King What-Soever-Youthink was dead, and that the princes must hasten back to Daybyday, where Really-Is would be crowned with the Magic Crown and become the Ruler of Allthetime.

All was hurry and confusion in the palace of Lookingahead as the guests made swift preparations for their journey. Quickly the word went throughout the city and many charming people came to express regret, to sympathize and to bid the young men good-speed and safe going on their homeward way. The princesses, Fancy and Imagination, were very sad at losing their pleasant companions; and the Chief High Priest of the Temple commanded services and offerings extraordinary to the god Itmightbe.

"And this, O Hadji," whispered the Voice of the Evening Wind, "is all of The Tale of The Uncrowned King that is given me to tell."

The evening song of leaf and blade, and flower and bird, and all their kind and kin, ceased to come through the open window into The Quiet Room. The low Voice of the Evening Wind no longer whispered to the Pilgrim as he lay upon his couch. Without the Temple the eventide was passing from over the silent land and over the silent sea.

For a little the Pilgrim waited; then rising from his couch, again he went to the open window, and lo! in the evening sky he saw the City Sometime in the Land of Yet-tocome. All the wondrous castles and palaces were there, marvelous in their beauty, glorious in their splendor, dazzling in their colors of emerald, rose and purple, of ruby, crimson and gold. From spire and dome, cupola and turret, tower and battlement the lights flashed and gleamed, while the

Pilgrim looked in wonder and in awe. And high above the city walls, that shone as burnished silver in the sun, rose the temple flaming like a ruby flame—the temple sacred to the god Itmightbe.

Slowly, slowly, the last of the twilight passed. Slowly, the graceful lines, the proud forms, the majestic piles of the city melted— melted, blurred and were lost even as are lost the form and loveliness of a snow flake on the sleeve. Slowly, slowly, the glorious colors faded as fade the flowers at the touch of frost. The lights went out. The darkness came. The city that is fairer than an angel's dream was gone.

*And the Third Voice was the
Voice of the Night*

And the Third Voice
was the
Voice of the Night

IT was full night when the Pilgrim turned again to seek his couch.

Without the Temple it was very still—dark and still. Very still was it within The Quiet Room, and the darkness that came stealing through the open window was a thick and heavy darkness. The Pilgrim lay upon his couch staring with blank, unseeing eyes into a blackness wherein there was not even a spot of gray to show where the window was.

And after a little there came out of the heavy darkness the sad, sad Voice of the Night.

Said the Voice: "To thee, O Hadji, I come from the Limitless Realm of the Past that begins this moment and reaches back even beyond the day of all beginnings. I speak from the Deeps Above. I tell of the Great That Was. I also am a Voice of Life, and mine it is to tell you yet more of The Tale of The Uncrowned King."

And this is the part of the Tale that was told by the Voice of the Night.

Now it happened, as things sometime so happen, that Really-Is lingered over long, saying good-bye to his friends in the City Sometime in the Land of Yetto-come; and that when he had lingered long with his friends he stayed yet longer with the beautiful princess, Imagination.

So it was that, while the prince was promising many promises and receiving in turn promises as many, his brother, Seemsto-Be, mounted and was well started on his journey before the heir to the throne of Allthetime was in the saddle. With the last good-bye spoken to his royal friends, the last promise promised to the fair princess, and the last farewell waved to the charming people, Really-Is urged his horse fast and faster, thinking thus to overtake his brother. But very soon Really-Is found that, fast as he rode his good horse Reality, Seemsto-Be on Appearance rode faster.

Greater and greater grew the distance between the two princes — farther and farther ahead rode Seemsto-Be; until at last, when the distance between them was such that he could no longer see his brother, Really-Is, the rightful heir to the throne of Allthetime, understood that Seemsto-Be was riding to win the Crown.

"For you must not forget, O Hadji," said the sad Voice of the Night, "that no one in Daybyday could tell the twins, Really-Is and Seemsto-Be, one from the other, and therefore, you see, the prince who first reached the Royal City would surely be proclaimed king."

Hard and fast, fast and hard, rode the two who raced for the Crown of Allthetime. But always Appearance the horse of Seemsto-Be, proved faster than Reality, the horse of Really-Is, and so the prince who was first born rode far behind.

Now just this side of the river that marks the end of the Land of Allthetime the road divides, the way to the left leading to the Brazen Gate called Chance, and the other, to the right, going straight to the Golden Gate, Opportunity. And just here it is, at the parting of the ways, that Wisdom lives in his little house beside the road. [80]

When Really-Is in turn arrived at this place, he dismounted from his tired horse, and approaching the little house, asked of Wisdom if he had seen one pass that way riding in great haste.

"Aye, that I have," replied Wisdom with a smile, "that I have, young sir, and many would say that it was yourself who rode so hard."

"It was my brother, good sir," replied the prince. "May I ask which way he went and how far he rides ahead?"

The old man, pointing, answered: "He took the road to the left there and he rides so far ahead that you cannot now overtake him this side the city walls."

"At least I must try to overtake him," answered the prince, and, thanking the old man, he turned quickly to mount his horse again.

But Wisdom cried, "Why so fast? Why so fast? Is not your brother's name Seemsto-Be? And are not you, Really-Is, the rightful heir to the throne of Allthetime?"

"It is indeed so, sir," replied the young man sadly. "I am Really-Is. I was born before my brother, Seemsto-Be, and am, therefore, the rightful heir to the Crown. Our father, King What-Soever-

Youthink, is dead, and I must hasten or my brother will be crowned king, for as you see, the people cannot tell us one from the other."

Then said Wisdom: "But you will gain nothing by haste, oh Really-Is,—nothing but time, and there is much of greater value than time to a King of Allthetime. Even now is Seemsto-Be entering the city. Even now is he by the people being hailed King. Therefore, tarry a while before you act and listen to my words."

So it was that Really-Is paused on his journey to sit awhile with Wisdom in the little house by the side of the road.

Then did Wisdom take from his shelves many a ponderous, time worn volume and read to the prince History, Prophecy and Law, revealing to him thus the Secret of the Magic of the Crown of All-thetime.

And from the last volume, that which Wisdom read to Really-Is was this: "Be it known, O who-soever readeth, that if any prince of the royal family Everyone enter the city Daybyday through the Brazen Gate called Chance, he shall be forever held unworthy of the throne and crown. In the sacred Law of All the Ages it is written that a King of Allthetime

may enter the Royal City only through the Golden Gate Opportunity."

Wisdom closed the book and returned this volume also to its place.

Really-Is arose to go.

"And what now is your mind, young sir?" asked Wisdom kindly.

Then Really-Is answered royally: "This you have taught me, O Wisdom—this is my mind: *The Crown is not the kingdom, nor is one King because he wears a crown.*"

Then did Wisdom with bowed head salute the True King. "And your will, Sire; may I know your Majesty's will?"

King Really-Is replied: "My will is this: that I myself obey the sacred Law of The Ages."

"And your brother, Sire, your brother, Seemsto-Be?"

"I will pity Seemsto-Be," replied The King in sorrow, "I will have much pity for that poor, foolish one."

"And peace will dwell in thy heart, O King of Allthetime," said Wisdom, "true peace and understanding."

Then Really-Is, alone and unattended, rode slowly on his way.

And Seemsto-Be, who rode so fast and so far ahead of Really-Is, and who paused not at the house

of Wisdom, entered the city Daybyday through the Brazen Gate
called Chance, and was received
by the people of many races, languages, names and religions as
their king.

With great tumult and shouting,
with grand processions and cere-
monies, the false prince ascended
the throne of Allthetime and was
crowned with the Magic Crown—
the Crown of which no one then
knew its magic, but knew only
that its magic was.

Then began such times as were
never before nor since seen in
Daybyday; with holiday after holiday for the people, with festivals

and parades, with carnivals and games, with feasting and dancing; until the chief occupation of the people was forgotten—until their many temples were empty, their many gods neglected; until with a fete extraordinary, Seemsto-Be decreed that there should be from henceforth and forever, in Daybyday, one temple only—one temple sacred to one god, the god Things-Are-Good-Enough.

"And this, O Hadji," said the sad Voice of the Night, "is all The Tale of The Uncrowned King that is given me to tell."

The Voice in the darkness ceased. The Pilgrim, rising,

groped his way to the window.

Without, all was dark with a thick darkness—all was still with a heavy stillness. Only the stars were in the Deeps Above. The stars so old, so ever new — only the stars. Lifting his face, the Pilgrim looked at the stars, and lo! as he looked, those whirling worlds of light shaped themselves into mighty letters, and the letters shaped themselves into words, until in the heavens the Pilgrim read the truth that Wisdom had given to Really-Is in the little house beside the road. *"The Crown is not the kingdom, nor is one King because he wears a crown."*

Then even as he stood the
Pilgrim saw the sad Night prepar-
ing to depart. Far away beyond
the stars the first faint light of the
morning touched the sky. Slowly
the world began to awake. Slowly
the message in the stars was lost
in the dawning greater light of A
New Day.

And the Fourth Voice was the Voice of the New Day.

And the
Fourth Voice
Was the Voice
of the New Day

IT was gray dawn when the
Pilgrim turned once more to
his couch in The Quiet Room.

Without the Temple, tree and bush and plant and grass were beginning to stir with fresh and joyous strength, while the clean air was rich with the smell of the earth life and filled with murmuring, twittering, whispering, morning calls. Through the open window, into The Quiet Room where the Pilgrim lay, the Bright Morning entered, and out of the Morning came the glad, glad Voice of the New Day.

Said this Voice to the Pilgrim: "To thee, O Hadji, I come from the Infinite Future. The interminable, eternal times that are to come, that begin but never end.

I cry from the Deeps Within. I call from the Great That Will Be. I, too, am a Voice of Life, and mine it is to complete for you The Tale of The Uncrowned King."

And this is the part of the Tale that the Voice of the New Day completed.

Really-Is, the true King of All-thetime, after leaving Wisdom in his little house beside the road, journeyed slowly and thoughtfully toward the Royal City Daybyday, along the way that leads to the Golden Gate Opportunity. And while the pretender, Seemsto-Be, was delighting the people with great feasts, and amusing them with all manner of festivals, parades and games, Really-Is, very quietly—so quietly that his brother did not know—entered the city and took up his abode in a tiny house under the walls of a deserted temple once sacred to the god Things-That-Ought-To-Be.

And so it was that when Seems-to-Be went forth from the royal palace to ride in grand procession, clothed in regal splendors, with the Crown upon his head, and surrounded by gorgeous soldiers of rank and pompous officials of state, with the royal trumpeters proclaiming his greatness and power and the multitude shouting

[98]

loud expressions of their loyalty,
Really-Is, the King, stood still beside the way, smiling, smiling sadly
at the pretty show.

And never did Really-Is neglect
to make his offering every morning in the temple sacred to the
god Things-That-Ought-To-Be;
though in secret he worshiped there
because of the decree of Seemsto-
Be. And no one told the false
ruler that his commandment was
broken, nor spoke to him the name
of his brother Really-Is.

But after a while, as time passed
by, things went not so gaily with
the impostor on the throne of
Allthetime. And it was the Crown

that did it—that wonderful Magic Crown.

The Court Fool noticed it first and made a jest about it, and Seemsto-Be laughed royally long and loud, and all the Court laughed with him, for the fool, Thinks-He-Is, is a most famous fool, the greatest that has ever been since the Father of Fools was born.

Next, the Lord Chief High Chamberlain noticed, and the Lord Chief High Chamberlain whispered to Seemsto-Be a most portentous whisper. And the portentous whisper of the Lord Chief High Chamberlain reached the ears of the Chief First Officer of State;

then passed from Officer of State to Officer of State until it reached the Chief Captain of the Guard, and soon the soldiers of the royal army and even the royal servants of the palace were whispering, whispering, whispering about the strange affair.

Then it was that Seemsto-Be sent throughout the kingdom, commanding in haste to the palace the most expert workers in gems and the most cunning workers in gold to be found in the Land of Allthetime.

It was true. The priceless jewels of the Magic Crown were losing their brilliancy. The precious gold of the Crown was becoming dull. Nor could all the skill of the workers in gems, all the craft of the workers in gold restore the beauty of the Crown or keep its fading splendor.

And so the whispers grew louder and louder until the people began to talk in low tones among themselves, questioning, questioning one another of the meaning of this thing. And at last the Royal Officers of State began to look with distrust and fear upon their ruler, who tried so hard to wear bravely his crown of tarnished gold and lusterless gems; and the soldiers came to look with doubt and fear upon the officers, who whispered so among themselves; and the people looked with suspicion and fear upon them all.

Without understanding, filled with dread and apprehension, worn with wracking worry, poor Seemsto-Be sought with honors, decorations, and distinguishing titles to hold the fast-failing confidence of his court and army, and with holidays more frequent, festivals more gay, games more interesting, and parades more gorgeous, tried to keep the waning loyalty of his people.

Now all this time, while the poor foolish pretender, Seemsto-

Be, was losing his power even as the beauty of the Magic Crown was fading, King Really-Is lived very quietly in his little house under the walls of the abandoned temple, and never did he fail to make his daily offering to his god, the god Things-That-Ought-To-Be. And always when his brother Seemsto-Be with the fading Crown upon his head, passed in gorgeous procession of state, surrounded by his distrustful officers, doubting soldiers and suspicious people, Really-Is smiled sadly and whispered to himself: "Poor Seemsto-Be, poor foolish one!"

So it was, that in all the Royal

City Daybyday, in the Land of Allthetime, peace and understanding dwelt only in the heart of this King.

And the people more and more came to love Really-Is, even as they more and more turned from Seemsto-Be, notwithstanding the holidays, feasts and parades. Little by little, they learned to watch daily for their King, and with the children would run to greet him. More and more the multitude pressed about Really-Is when he stood quietly in the street, watching Seemsto-Be pass by in the splendid chariot of state. More and more the people went daily with

Really-Is to worship in the temple sacred to the god Things-That-Ought-To-Be.

So the time came at last when the Magic Crown, tarnished and dull, seemed but a mockery, fit only for the rubbish heap; when the Officers of State spoke aloud their doubts and fears and the soldiers were openly disobedient; when the people, as the pretender passed through the city streets, no longer shouted aloud expressions of their loyalty, but, with dark looks of doubt and anger, stood silent, or laughed in mocking glee.

And Seemsto-Be grew afraid.

Then in secret the false prince went alone to the house of his brother the King and prostrated himself humbly.

"What is your wish, my brother?" asked Really-Is, kindly, "make known to me your request."

And Seemsto-Be taking heart at the gentleness of Really-Is answered: "This is my wish, O King—my brother, this is my request; that you come to dwell with me in the royal palace, that you share with me the throne. Twins we are, sons of our royal father, of the royal family Everyone. Therefore let us rule together the Land of Allthetime.

Answered Really-Is. "By your coming to me, Seemsto-Be, I know that you, too, at last have learned the Secret of the Magic of the Crown. What of the Crown, brother?"

And the pretender replied: "No one can tell us one from the other. You only shall wear the Crown; then for us both will its glory come again and remain, then will all be well."

But King Really-Is answered sadly: "O my brother, that which you ask cannot be. In the Law of the Ages it is written that a King of Allthetime cannot, if he would, share his throne and power with one who is false, else would he himself be held unworthy I have seen your wretchedness, my brother; I have seen and I have pitied."

Then Seemsto-Be went sadly out from the presence of his brother, the King, and the next morning they found him dead on the steps of the temple sacred to the god Things-Are-Good-Enough.

And now with great tumult and shouting the people gathered to do homage to Really-Is. And never was there seen in Daybyday such a multitude. From the uttermost parts of Allthetime they came, for the word of his life had

gone far, far abroad and all the
world that is, gathered to do him
honor.

And it happened, when all was
ready for Really-Is to ascend the
throne, and the royal trumpeters
had lifted their trumpets ready to
proclaim him King of Allthetime,
with the vast multitude breath-
less, ready at the signal of the
trumpets to break forth in a great,
glad shout, "Long live the king,"
and the Lord Chief High Chamberlain turned to take the Magic
Crown from the hands of the High
Priest of Things-That-Ought-To-
Be, that even as he turned the
Crown vanished, and lo! there

was in the hands of the priest, nothing.

In consternation the Lord Chief High Chamberlain whispered to the royal high officials about him, asking what should be done. In consternation, the royal high officials whispered among themselves. In consternation they whispered back to the Chamberlain.

And this was their whisper: "Ask the King."

Really-Is, when he was asked what should be done, answered with a smile: *"The Crown is not the kingdom, nor is one King because he wears a Crown."*

And the people, when the

trumpets made it known that there was no crown and declared the word of Really-Is, with one voice cried loudly: "Really-Is is King! Really-Is needs no Crown! Long live Really-Is, our King!"

Thus the True King ascended the throne of Allthetime, and the trumpeters trumpeted loudly many times: "Long live the king who needs no crown!" and with a great shout the people answered again many times: "Long live our Uncrowned King! Long live our Uncrowned King!"

"And this, O Hadji," said the glad Voice of the New Day, "is how it came to be that in the

days that now are, there is, in this
Royal City Daybyday, in the
wonderful Land of Allthetime, no
crown.

And this also you must know,
that in the reign of Really-Is the
people of Daybyday have more and
more turned from their many
gods to worship only the god of
their King, until there is left now
of the many deserted temples
only ruins, and of the many gods
of the many people of many races,
languages and names only one, the
god of Really-Is, Things-That-
Ought-To-Be. The mighty Wall
that was built, they thought,
on the foundations of the world,

when there was no longer a crown
to keep, of its own great weight
fell. And the Royal City Daybyday, in the reign of Really-Is, is
extending its borders more and
more, until there are those who
think that with the City Sometime
it will soon be one, and then they
say that the promises made by
Really - Is and the Princess of
Yettocome will be fulfilled and
that the glory and splendor of
their reign will fill the world.

"But of that, O Hadji," said
the glad Voice of the New Day,
"I cannot tell you now. I have
finished The Tale of The Uncrowned King."

The Voice that was in the
Morning ceased. The Quiet Room
was filled with light. Quickly the
Pilgrim arose and going to the
window saw in all its glory the
New Day.

Every leaf of the tall trees,
every blade and every inwoven
flower in the velvet carpet of
green, wore beads of shining crystal that sparkled and glittered in
radiant splendor. Every tiny rip-
ple that ran on the Beautiful Sea
was a line of silver flame. And
in the overhead ocean of pearly
light, floated glowing banks of
orange, and scarlet and gold, while,
to the Pilgrim, bird and tree and

plant and flower and wave and cloud seemed to join in one glad triumphant shout: "Long live Really-Is! Long live The Uncrowned King!"

Then the Pilgrim who had paid The Price, who had fulfilled The Law of the Pilgrimage, who had asked of Thyself, the Keeper of the Temple of Truth, "Why," went to lay his offering on the altar to the god That-Never-Can Change.

And his offering was Himself.

THE END

THE CALLING OF
DAN MATTHEWS

"Mr. Wright has written other novels, but this one is so strong and wholesome, so attractive as literature, so interesting as a story, so artistic in preparation, that it wins increasing favor as one gets into it."—*Buffalo Evening News.*

"Mr. Wright has the gift of knowing people well and of being able to set out their characteristics so clearly that his reader also knows them well."—*Chicago Journal.*

"It is a privilege to meet the people whom the author allows you to know. They are worth while; and to cry and feel with them, get into the fresh, sweet atmosphere with which the writer surrounds them—and above all, to understand Dan Matthews and to go with him in his unfoldment—these will repay you."—*Portland Spectator.*

"Harold Bell Wright has done a fine big piece of work. * * * One might quote at length from the old doctor's homely philosophy. The book can not be read without the keenest enjoyment and at the end of the story one feels that the people are old friends, real flesh and blood characters, so human are they all."—*San Francisco Call.*

The Shepherd of the Hills

"There are many bits of excellent description in the course of the story, and an atmosphere as fresh and sweet and free from modern grime as one would breathe on the Ozark trails themselves."—*New York Times.*

"Amidst all the ordinary literature of the day, it is as a pure, white stone set up along a dreary road of unending monotony."—*Buffalo Courier.*

"It is filled with laughs and tears, this beautiful story, and no one can help laughing or crying in turn, if his heart is right."—*Pueblo Chieftain.*

"It is a heart-stirring story. A tale to bring laughter and tears; a story to be read and read again."—*Grand Rapids Herald.*

That Printer of Udell's

"Altogether an estimable story."—*New York Sun.*

"Done to the life."—*Chicago Tribune.*

"Well written and decidedly interesting."—*New York Times.*

"A thoroughly good novel."—*Boston Globe.*

"Wrings tears and laughter."—*Record-Herald, Chicago.*

"Absorbing, thoughtful novel."—*Kansas City Journal.*

"Full of movement and passion."—*Standard, Chicago.*

"It is human to the very core."—*Nashville American.*

"Excellent character creation."—*St. Louis Republic.*

"Wholesome and strengthening."—*Albany Press.*

"Rich in humor and good sense."—*Philadelphia Telegraph*

"Full of thrilling interest and moral heroism."—*Pittsburg Dispatch.*

"Many well drawn characters."—*Washington Post.*

"Has not a peer in English fiction."—*Providence Telegram*

"It is strong and wholesome."—*Chicago Post.*

"Not a chapter that is not interesting."—*St. Paul News.*

"It is a fascinating story."—*Portland Telegram.*

"It should be read to be understood."—*Grand Rapids Herald.*

"The reader's interest is stirred to its very depths"—*Omaha World-Herald.*